TRAPPED IN THE TEMPLE

AN UNOFFICIAL MINECRAFTER MYSTERIES SERIES

BOOK FIVE

TRAPPED IN THE TEMPLE
AN UNOFFICIAL MINECRAFTER MYSTERIES SERIES
BOOK FIVE

Winter Morgan

Sky Pony Press
New York

Copyright © 2018 by Hollan Publishing, Inc.

Minecraft® is a registered trademark of Notch Development AB.

The Minecraft game is copyright © Mojang AB.

Sky Pony Press books may be purchased in bulk at special discounts for sales promotion, corporate gifts, fund-raising, or educational purposes. Special editions can also be created to specifications. For details, contact the Special Sales Department, Sky Pony Press, 307 West 36th Street, 11th Floor, New York, NY 10018 or info@skyhorsepublishing.com.

Sky Pony® is a registered trademark of Skyhorse Publishing, Inc.®, a Delaware corporation.

Minecraft® is a registered trademark of Notch Development AB.
The Minecraft game is copyright © Mojang AB.

Visit our website at www.skyponypress.com.

10 9 8 7 6 5 4 3 2 1

Library of Congress Cataloging-in-Publication Data is available on file.

Cover design by Brian Peterson
Cover photo by Megan Miller

Print ISBN: 978-1-5107-3191-2
Ebook ISBN: 978-1-5107-3197-4

Printed in the United States of America

TABLE OF CONTENTS

TRAPPED IN THE TEMPLE

THE UNOFFICIAL MINECRAFTER MYSTERIES SERIES

BOOK FIVE

1

FLASH SALE

Billy's arms hurt as he carried two heavy cases filled with potions. "I've worked at the stand for a very long time, and I've helped you bring many things to town, but I've never felt anything this heavy before. My arms are sore. What do you have in these cases? Why are they so heavy?"

Edison, who was also lugging two large cases to town, explained, "After helping you on the great treasure hunt, I found that I had so many extra ingredients and was able to brew a ton of potions. Since I lack the room to store all of them, I had an idea that I'd have a big sale today, which would help me make some room for the new potions I'd like to brew."

Billy put the cases on the blocky ground, taking an unannounced break. "I hope the sale is a success, because then we get to carry an empty case or two on the way back."

Edison smiled. "Me too. I'm sorry the cases are hard to carry."

Billy picked them back up. "It's okay. I just wish you had warned me."

"Again, I'm sorry. I should have, but we're almost there," Edison said. He stopped when he saw the line of customers.

"Wow, I've never seen so many people in line before. Word must have spread about your sale." Billy picked up the pace and made his way to the stand. He placed the potions down while a horde of people crowded around him.

"What are you selling?" a woman dressed in red shirt and pants asked Billy. "Tell me what's on sale."

Edison controlled the crowd while Billy set up the stand. "Please give us some space. We will have all of the potions ready to sell in a few minutes. Everything is on sale."

A man in a denim jacket tried to cut to the front of the line, but the woman dressed in red called out, "What are you doing? You can't cut to the front of the line. That's not fair."

"I need a potion of Water Breathing, and I want to make sure I get it before it runs out," he announced.

"We all want different potions, but we have to wait our turn. We arrived very early so we could get all of the potions we needed," another customer screamed from the center of the line.

The man in the denim jacket pleaded, "But you

don't understand, this is urgent. I need it more than anyone else."

"Then you should have gotten here earlier," someone screamed, and the others agreed.

No matter how much he pleaded his case for getting a better spot on line, nobody seemed to care. The person knew it was pointless to continue and made his way to the back of the line. When he reached the end of the line, Edison announced the stand was officially open and the sale had begun.

As the words "it's open for business" fell from Edison's lips, the first person in line began to list the potions, and Billy pulled them from the cases. The list seemed endless, and Edison realized he should have made a cap on how many bottles each person could purchase from the stand. He wasn't sure if he could create this new rule on the spot. He watched as a group of people walked to the back of the line, and then he looked down at his case of potion. If he didn't cap the amount of potions each person could buy, he wouldn't even be able to serve the people who had been waiting on line for hours.

"A potion of Water Breathing," the customer said, and he didn't seem to take a breath while continuing to list other potions.

"I'm sorry," said Edison. "There's a limit. Only three bottles of potion per customer."

"What?" the infuriated customer hollered. "I've waited here since daybreak. I left my home when the hostile mobs were still forming. I had to defeat a spider jockey. After that, two Endermen teleported in front of me, and I had to sprint into a nearby ocean. This wasn't an easy journey, and I'm not sure I would have taken it if I knew I was only getting a discount on three bottles of potion. It's just not fair."

Edison understood the man's point and apologized. "I should have mentioned this earlier. However, this is the rule. Please tell me the three bottles you'd like to purchase."

The man listed the three bottles, and the new system seemed to work smoothly until the person in the denim jacket reached Edison and Billy.

"I want everything you have left," said the man in the denim jacket.

Edison looked down at the case. There were only seven potions left, but he wasn't going to give them all to this person.

"We have a rule in place, and we can't make exceptions," explained Billy.

The person said, "I'll take three bottles of the potion of Water Breathing."

"Okay." Edison handed him the potions, and the person gave him an emerald.

Before the stranger walked away, he screamed, "Here's a warning to all of you waiting in line. Everyone should get a potion of Water Breathing. We're all going to need it."

"What are you talking about?" asked Billy.

"There is trouble brewing in the Overworld. You'll see. Things are going to start happening soon."

"What sort of things are going to be happening?" questioned Edison.

"I can't tell you, but you'll see for yourself," he replied while clutching three bottles of potion of Water Breathing and scurrying out of Farmer's Bay.

"What was that about?" asked Billy.

"I have no idea," said Edison. He sold his remaining four bottles of potion.

2

AN EASY CASE

Edison couldn't stop thinking about the incident that occurred during the flash sale. It had been a few weeks since the stranger in the denim jacket arrived in town, warning everyone they should stock up on potion of Water Breathing, and nothing had happened. Although Billy said the person was just trying to get attention, every time Edison brewed potions, he'd make a few extra bottles of the potion of Water Breathing. He was in the middle of brewing a new batch when he noticed he had run out of pufferfish and Nether wart, and he began to worry. He counted the bottles of potion. He had twelve bottles of the potion of Water Breathing, and he knew he had to find ingredients to make more. Since that mad outburst from the man in the denim jacket, this potion had become his top seller.

"Edison." Billy opened his front door.

"Come in." Edison invited him in as he stood by

7

his brewing stand at work. "I have to go to the Nether and then fishing for pufferfish. I ran out of ingredients for the potion of Water Breathing because people keep requesting it now." But Edison stopped talking when he saw a woman wearing a sparkly purple dress and a tiara standing behind Billy.

"Hi." She smiled. "My name is Princess Hannah. I've come a very far distance to see you."

"Me?" asked Edison as he left his brewing stand and walked toward them. "Why?"

"I heard that you and Billy are the best detectives in the Overworld," she explained.

"That's flattering. We also work with our friend Anna. We're a team, but we're not officially detectives. We just solve cases that affect the citizens of Farmer's Bay and Verdant Valley," explained Edison.

"Didn't you help save the brewing competition and the great treasure hunt?" asked Princess Hannah.

"Well, yes." Edison wanted to explain that he never intended to become a detective and that those cases had found him, but he decided that he should listen to Princess Hannah and find out why she was in Farmer's Bay seeking out his help. "Can you tell me what you want me to help you with?"

"I lost Scooter." Her eyes filled with tears.

Puddles meowed, and Edison pulled some fish out of his inventory and fed the hungry ocelot as he asked, "Who is Scooter?"

"My ocelot." Tears streamed down her cheeks as she looked at Puddles.

Edison thought about how much he loved Puddles and how upset he'd be if Puddles went missing.

"That's awful," he said. "I will help you find Scooter."

"I'll help too," said Billy.

"I'm so happy," Princess Hannah exclaimed. "When can we leave?"

Edison looked out the window; it was almost nighttime. "Where do you live?"

"I live with my family in the desert. In a desert temple," Princess Hannah replied.

"I think we should leave first thing in the morning," said Edison. "I have some work I have to finish here, but feel free to stay here. I have room for you."

Billy said, "We should also ask Anna to join us. She is very good at helping us solve cases."

"Good idea," Edison agreed. "Maybe we should TP to Anna's house and see if she wants to go."

The trio TPed, and they arrived in front of Anna's door as the sky grew dark. She invited them in, and they explained that they were going to help Princess Hannah find her ocelot, but before Edison was able to explain the situation, an arrow flew through the sky and landed in Edison's back.

"Ouch!" He screamed out in pain as the arrow pierced his unarmored body.

Princess Hannah turned around to see a horde of skeletons with their bows and arrows aimed at the group. Four foul-smelling zombies lumbered down the dark pathway beside the bony beasts.

"We're being attacked," Edison said as he tried to hold his breath so he wouldn't breathe in the fetid odor emanating from the undead beasts that walked toward them.

Edison pulled out his sword, lunging at one of the zombies, ripping into its oozing flesh. Princess Hannah quickly placed her shiny diamond armor over her purple dress, grabbed an enchanted diamond sword from her inventory, and attacked the zombies.

Billy and Anna focused on annihilating the skeletons, slamming their diamond swords into the bony beasts. The sounds of clanging bones were deafening. Billy tried to avoid getting struck by the skeleton's arrows as they skillfully attempted to destroy the two skeletons. The skeletons were strong, and no matter how many times they swung their enchanted diamond swords at the bony beasts, the weapons didn't seem to weaken them.

"Use potion," Edison called out as he watched their battle unfold from the corner of his eye while fighting the foul-smelling zombies himself.

Billy pulled out a potion and splashed the skeletons, finally weakening the beasts enough to destroy them. Once the skeletons were gone, Billy and Anna picked up the bones that dropped on the ground.

With great force, Edison ripped into another zombie. He almost threw up when he got a whiff of the decaying flesh, but he held his breath and leaped at the weakened zombie. Princess Hannah stood by his side as she slayed the remaining zombie. Once they obliterated the undead pests and picked up the rotten flesh they had dropped, Anna called out, "Let's get into my house quickly. We have to make sure we aren't attacked by any other hostile mobs."

The gang rushed into Anna's house. As they crowded into her small living room, she asked, "What are you guys doing here?"

Princess Hannah told Anna the story of the missing ocelot. Anna remarked, "That's awful. Why don't we travel to the desert tomorrow and help you look? This sounds like an easy case."

Anna had just enough room for all four of them, and she showed them to their beds. As Edison climbed into the bed, he thought about Anna calling the case easy. He hadn't been solving crimes for that long, but he had never come across an easy case. However, he had to admit that a missing ocelot seemed to be a solvable problem.

As Edison drifted off to bed, he wondered if they should trust Princess Hannah. Perhaps she was tricking them. Maybe there wasn't a simple case of a missing ocelot, and she was leading them into a trap. He questioned why she would want to trick them and wondered why he was suspicious of this new person who had come to them for help. As he closed his eyes, he heard Princess Hannah unleash a bloodcurdling scream.

"Stop! Help! Please don't destroy the Overworld. I'll go under the water." Princess Hannah wailed as she sat up in bed.

Anna rushed to her side, asking, "Are you okay?"

Princess Hannah rubbed her eyes. "I must have been having a bad dream."

Edison stayed up all night; he couldn't fall asleep, even when the princess went back to bed. Every time he closed his eyes, he remembered the words Princess Hannah screamed in her sleep: "I'll go under water." He knew this wasn't a simple case of a missing ocelot.

3
EMPTY

The sun peeked through the window, and Edison sat up in the bed as he heard Princess Hannah talking with Anna.

"You had a very bad dream last night," Anna explained, but Princess Hannah didn't remember it at all. Edison wanted to confront Princess Hannah about her dream. What did she mean when she said she'd go underwater? But now there didn't seem to be a point, because Princess Hannah didn't seem to remember screaming anything aloud in the middle of the night.

"Edison," Billy called to his friend, "would you like a piece of cake?"

Billy was making breakfast for everyone. Princess Hannah paced around the small kitchen, her mouth full of cake as she wiped tears from her eyes.

"Don't worry," Edison reassured her. "We will find Scooter."

She swallowed her cake and said, "Thank you, can we leave soon? I just want to get back to the desert."

"Yes." Edison smiled. "We can go now."

"Great, I'll lead the way," said Princess Hannah.

"We should make sure we have stocked inventories before we set out for the desert," suggested Billy.

While searching through his inventory, Edison remembered that he was out of Nether wart and puffer-fish, and although he hated traveling to the Nether, he knew he must go there after they solved this case. He also had to find time to go fishing, but first he had to help Princess Hannah find her pet ocelot.

The trip to the desert was longer than they expected, and it wasn't until they reached the swamp that Billy suggested they TP to the desert.

"That's a great idea," said Princess Hannah. "I have no idea why we didn't think of it before." Princess Hannah tried to TP to her brother Prince Elias, but it didn't work. "That's strange," she remarked. "I guess I will try to TP to my parents. Maybe he is traveling and not in the desert." Princess Hannah tried to TP to her parents, but that didn't work either.

Princess Hannah was worried. "I hope everyone is okay."

Anna said, "I'm sure they're fine. Let's just travel there. It isn't too much farther, right?"

The princess took out her map and pointed to the desert. "It's not that far." Edison looked at the map and saw they had to travel through a forest to get to the desert. The sun was starting to set, and a full moon was visible in the sky. Two bats flew close to Edison's neck.

"Watch out," Billy warned as three more bats flew toward Edison.

"I think we should build a house," said Princess Hannah, and she apologized. "I didn't realize this journey would take as long as it did. When I traveled to Farmer's Bay, I ran the entire way, and it took much less time."

"It's okay, there's no rush." Billy smiled and took out some wood planks from his inventory and began crafting a house on the shore of the swampy water.

Edison wasn't as relaxed as Billy. He felt there was a reason to rush. He had to gather a bunch of ingredients for his potions, and he also had to work at his potion stand. He never asked to be a detective, and this new side career was taking time away from his other responsibilities. But he didn't say anything as he helped construct the house.

Boing. Boing. Boing. Three green, boxy slimes hopped along the swampy shoreline.

"Oh no!" Princess Hannah called out as she grabbed her sword and sliced into one of the slimes; it broke into two smaller slimes. Edison ripped into a large, boxy slime and also created two smaller slimes. Anna leaped at the final remaining large slime. The small slimes attacked the group. Using their swords, they were able to defeat the boxy creature and pick up the slimeballs. Edison said, "We can craft slime blocks."

"We have to finish building this house. We have to hurry," said Billy as he stacked wood panels and tried to craft a house before other hostile mobs lurking in the swamp tried to attack them, but it was too late. A shrill laugh filled the air, and a witch dashed toward them clutching a potion.

"A witch!" screamed Edison.

The purple-robed witch splashed Princess Hannah with a potion of Slowness and then pulled out a second bottle of potion, dousing Edison with a potent poisonous potion, which weakened him and left him with one heart. He could barely stand, and he used his last bit of strength to pull a vial of potion from his inventory. He drank the potion of Healing as he lunged at the witch, striking the evil swamp dweller with his diamond sword.

The witch quickly pulled another potion from her inventory and splashed it on Edison. He felt incredibly weak and wondered if the potion of Healing he had brewed was strong enough. He leaped at the witch one more time, but she splashed him again, and he lost all of his hearts. He awoke in his bed with Puddles by his side.

"I have to help Princess Hannah find her missing ocelot," he said to Puddles, although he was fairly certain the ocelot didn't understand what he had said. He sat up in bed and was ready to TP to the swamp to be reunited with his friends when he heard the moaning of zombies outside his front door.

"Help!" Peyton hollered. "There's a zombie invasion!"

Edison drank two bottles of potion to regain his strength, and dressed in diamond armor, he raced outside.

4

BATTLES IN THE NIGHT

"**H**elp!" Erin cried as six zombies crowded around her.

Peyton annihilated three zombies and rushed to her friend's side as she struck the smelly zombies with her diamond sword.

"How long has this been going on?" asked Edison as he fought zombies alongside Erin and Peyton.

"All night. Where have you been?" asked Erin as she sliced into a zombie's arm.

"I was in the swamp. A princess asked me to help her find her missing ocelot," Edison explained as he destroyed a zombie.

The trio tirelessly battled a sea of zombies. Using a combination of potions and their swords, they were able to destroy all of the zombies that spawned in the middle of the night in Farmer's Bay.

The battle lasted the night, and sweat dripped down

Edison's face and blurred his vision as he slammed his sword into another zombie. The fight was tireless. Every time he destroyed a zombie, another would show up. It was getting lighter out, and Edison knew the zombies wouldn't be able to survive much longer.

As the sun rose, Erin said, "I have a feeling something bad is happening in the Overworld."

"Why do you say that?" asked Edison.

"This was an intense battle," she explained. "It lasted a lot longer than normal. I find that when these prolonged mob invasions happen, it isn't by accident."

Edison pondered what Erin had said and worried she was correct. He also recalled the man at the potion stand who prophesized there would be trouble in the Overworld and everyone should have extra potions of Water Breathing. However, he couldn't focus on what this man had said, and even Erin's comment, because he was committed to a case, and he had to solve it.

He rushed back to his house, fed Puddles, and sorted through his inventory to make sure he had what he needed for his trip back to meet his friends. He TPed to Billy's location and was surprised to see he was still in the swamp. Edison had thought they'd be closer to the desert.

"I didn't think you guys would still be in the swamp," said Edison.

Anna sipped milk and then said, "Last night was awful. We battled three witches. It was intense."

"And there were more slimes," added Billy.

"We were fighting hostile mobs until the sun came

up," said Princess Hannah, "but hopefully we'll be able to leave for the desert now."

"When I was destroyed and spawned in my bed, I awoke as Farmer's Bay was in the middle of a zombie invasion. I spent the entire night battling zombies," said Edison.

"Wow," Billy wondered aloud, "maybe these two invasions are related."

"I don't know," said Edison, "but we should travel to the desert. We have an entire day to get there, and we want to arrive before nightfall. We want time to be prepared if there are any other attacks."

Everyone agreed, and they set out to travel to the desert. As they traveled through the lush forest biome, Princess Hannah led the way and tried to clear a path for the rest of the group.

"We can't get lost in the leaves," she warned. "These paths get very thick with leaves, and sometimes we lose each other."

Edison spotted something rustling in the leaves and stopped. "Guys, do you see that?"

He was shocked when there was no response. "Hello? Billy?"

Silence.

"Princess Hannah? Anna? Where are you?"

Again he heard no reply. Edison was in the middle of the forest, and he could see the leaves rustling again. His heart beat faster as he made one last attempt to call out to his friends, but there was no response.

Edison stood still and took a deep breath. He

wanted to find out what was rustling in the leaves. He assumed it was a wolf and pulled out a bone to tame it. He walked slowly and approached the patch in the forest where he had seen the leaves move, then walked into the thick of the leaves. He looked down, but there wasn't a wolf.

"Hello," a voice called out.

This startled Edison. He looked in the direction of the voice and was stunned to see the man from the potion stand. The man, dressed in a denim jacket, said "I told you there was going to be trouble. It's time to live under the water."

"What are you talking about?" Edison asked calmly. He wanted all of the facts before he worried the Overworld was really in trouble.

"The battles last night were the first sign," the man declared. "You will see, it will just get worse. This is only the beginning."

"The beginning of what?"

The man laughed. "The end."

"The end of the Overworld?" questioned Edison. "But why?"

"There are people who want to end the universe," he explained, and before the man could say anything else, he pulled a potion of Invisibility out from his inventory, splashed it on himself, and disappeared.

"Edison," Billy called out as he sprinted toward his friend.

"Where were you?" asked Edison.

"I can ask you the same question. I turned around

and you were gone, and so were the others," replied Billy.

"Have you found Anna and Princess Hannah?" questioned Edison.

"No, you were the first person I found," he explained.

"We have to find them," said Edison, and as they walked through the narrow path through the dense forest, Edison told Billy about running into the man from the potion stand.

"I know a lot of strange things have been happening," remarked Billy, "but that doesn't mean what this man said is true. He could be trying to trick us. We don't even know his name."

"My name is Andrew," a voice called out, "and I'm telling you that the Overworld is in serious trouble."

"Why?" asked Billy.

There was no response. Andrew had disappeared again.

"What is wrong with this guy?" questioned Edison. "He keeps popping up and warning us of destruction, but he offers no details."

"I told you," Billy said with a laugh. "He's just trying to trick us."

Edison was about to speak when he heard Anna and Princess Hannah call out his name.

"We found you!" Anna yelled.

"Let's go to the desert before it gets dark," said Princess Hannah as they hurried through the forest toward the sunny, treeless desert biome.

5

DESERT FINDS

"We're almost there," said Princess Hannah.

They rushed past cacti and over a sand dune toward the grand desert temple with its orange and blue terracotta design. Princess Hannah picked up speed as she raced through the doors of the desert temple.

"Mom! Dad! Elias!" she called out, but she was met with silence. She sprinted throughout the temple, but nobody was there.

"Where are they?" she asked her new friends, but she knew they couldn't answer her question.

"Meow." The sound of an ocelot broke the silence. Scooter walked into the grand foyer, and the princess leaned down and fed it raw fish.

"You're back." She smiled at the ocelot.

"That was the easiest case we've ever solved," joked Billy.

They heard a sound in the temple, and Edison raced to investigate. He looked around, but he couldn't figure out where it was coming from. Edison stared at the ground. He looked over at Billy and said, "It sounded like it was coming from the ground."

Billy touched the sandstone ground, but there was nothing there.

Princess Hannah rushed in. "Did you find them?

"No," replied Billy.

"My family seems to be missing," the princess said.

"I'm sure there is a reason they aren't here," Billy reassured the princess.

"Maybe your family is just in town?" suggested Anna. "Should we go there?"

"That's a good idea, but I think we should also see if they are at a neighbor's house," said Billy.

"There aren't many neighbors here," explained Princess Hannah. "There's a small town, but it's on the other side of the village."

"Let's go to the village and then the town," said Edison.

"Okay," Princess Hannah said. She finished feeding the ocelot, and they set out to the desert village.

The village was quite busy, and the main street had a library, a smithy, and other shops. Edison wondered who the alchemist was in this desert village. As they explored the village and searched for Princess Hannah's family, the robed librarian walked down the block and spotted Princess Hannah. "Hannah," the librarian called out, "where have you been?"

"I was in Farmer's Bay. I wanted to seek out these detectives to help me find Scooter, my missing ocelot. When we arrived here we found Scooter, but we couldn't find my family."

"Nobody has seen them in a few days," said the librarian. "I thought you were with them."

"Do you have any idea where they might have gone?" asked Edison. He was in full detective mode. Obviously this wasn't going to be a simple case of trying to find a missing ocelot, which had already been found. Now he had to find her family.

"No, but something strange happened here last night," said the librarian.

"What?" asked Anna.

The librarian didn't have a chance to reply because the blacksmith rushed out of his shop and screamed, "Help!"

"Are you okay?" asked the librarian.

"No." The blacksmith's voice shook. "Someone just came into my shop and stole iron and gold."

"What? Where are they?" Anna questioned as she raced into the blacksmith's shop.

The rest of the gang followed her, but the shop was empty. Edison asked, "Where is the thief?"

"He sprinkled some potion on himself and disappeared," explained the blacksmith.

"How much did he steal?" Anna began to take notes. She assumed everything had to be tied into the case, and she wanted as much information as possible.

"He took all of my gold and iron." The blacksmith

pointed to his empty shelves. "It was odd because he was so nice at first. He talked to me about the attack last night, and then when I handed him all of the items he requested and I told him how much it would cost, he took out a sword and told me he had no money to pay me. Then he splashed a potion of Invisibility on himself and disappeared with all of the precious metals."

"What did he look like?" asked Edison.

"He had black hair, and he wore a blue denim jacket," said the blacksmith.

"A denim jacket!" exclaimed Billy. "It must be Andrew!"

"The strange thing is that he apologized before he disappeared," said the blacksmith.

"We have to find him," said Edison.

"How?" questioned Anna. "Do we know anything about him besides his name?"

"No," Edison replied, "but I have a feeling he is connected with the attacks that took place in the Overworld last night."

"Remember how he told us that everyone needs a potion of Water Breathing?" Billy said. Then he told everyone how he first met Andrew at the potion stand, when he declared the Overworld was going to be attacked and everyone should have potions of Water Breathing.

"You have to find this man and stop him," said the blacksmith.

The librarian agreed. "This thief can't get away with his crime."

"But what about my family?" Princess Hannah cried. "They're missing, and everyone is concerned with finding this thief."

"I will help you find your parents," Edison reassured Princess Hannah. "I promised you I would. And we will find them before we start our search for Andrew."

"Thank you," said Princess Hannah, "but where should we start looking for them?"

Edison paused. He didn't have an answer to that question, but he had to think of something. "I think we should search the desert temple for any clues. We rushed through there, and we never properly investigated."

Anna put her hand through her purple hair and said, "Yes, I agree, that sounds like the best plan. We promise we will help you find them."

"Thank you," Princess Hannah told the group.

The group charged back to the desert temple, but as they reached the entrance, they heard a familiar voice call out.

"Stop!" the voice screamed. "Don't go in there!"

Edison turned around, saw Andrew, and yelled, "Why?"

6

BACK IN THE VALLEY

Scooter the ocelot stood on the steps in front of the desert temple and meowed. Princess Hannah called out to her pet, "I'm back. It's all going to be okay." She turned around when she heard Andrew scream her name.

"Hannah! You can't go in there!" Andrew hollered.

Princess Hannah pulled out her diamond sword and raced toward Andrew. She held the sword close to his unarmored chest. "This is my house, you thief. Why can't I go inside?"

"I didn't mean to steal. I'm not a bad person. You need to follow me," he said. "I know where your family is. They're trapped in a dungeon. The person who trapped them booby-trapped your house with command blocks."

The gang shot a series of questions at Andrew.

"How do you know?" asked Edison.

"Where are they?" asked Princess Hannah.

"Where is the dungeon?" asked Billy.

Anna asked the final question, and it hung in the air for a while. "Why should we trust you?"

"If you don't trust me, go into the desert temple. But you'll all be destroyed," Andrew replied.

Edison didn't believe Andrew and walked toward the desert temple's door. Then Princess Hannah called out, "Edison! Stop!"

Edison paused in front of the large desert temple. "What? You're listening to him?"

Princess Hannah said, "Where is the dungeon?"

"It's in the desert. Follow me," he said. He scurried deeper into the beige-colored desert, past cacti and a few bushes. A gold rabbit hopped past them, and Edison almost tripped over the bunny that blended into the sand.

"That bunny was camouflaged," he said as he stumbled and steadied himself. Billy laughed, but Princess Hannah didn't even turn around and ask if he was okay. She was too busy trailing behind Andrew.

Edison couldn't believe this desert was so massive. He had traveled to other deserts before, but he had never seen a biome this large. The lack of shade made the hot sun even stronger than normal. Sweat fell off of Edison's face as he sprinted to keep up with the others. "Where is this dungeon?" he asked.

"Not far," Andrew told them.

Anna asked Andrew, "Who has them trapped in the dungeon?"

"Hal. He's the most powerful hacker in the universe. He has created glitches and caused attacks throughout the Overworld. Your family was about to confront him because he was behind Scooter's disappearance. Scooter wasn't the only ocelot missing, and when your parents found out that all the residents in the desert had lost their ocelots, your brother Elias began his own investigation. It was during this investigation that he met Hal."

"How do you know about Hal?" asked Edison.

"I've known about Hal for a long time. I have been chasing him and trying to stop his attacks. That was why I was at the sale in your town. I was trying to warn everyone about the upcoming destruction. If I'm not able to stop Hal, we will have a serious issue in the Overworld. He has a grand plan that will destroy all of the biomes in the Overworld except the underwater biome."

"Why would he leave that biome?" asked Billy.

"I think he's storing all of his loot in an ocean monument," said Andrew.

"Wow. How did you find out about Hal?" asked Anna.

"I told you, I have been chasing him for a long time. I encountered him when he attacked me."

"When?" asked Edison.

"A while ago, I was—"

Andrew was interrupted when a man with gray hair and glasses spawned in front of them. The man leaped at Andrew and splashed a bottle of potion at him, and Andrew disappeared.

"Who are you?" Edison asked as he pointed his diamond sword at the gray-haired man.

The man didn't answer. Instead he slammed a diamond sword into Edison's side, and Edison cried out in pain. Anna raced to Edison and handed him some milk to restore the hearts he lost from the attack. Billy lunged at the mysterious man, but as he swung his sword at the older man, the sword disappeared.

"What?" Billy looked at his empty hand in disbelief.

Anna and Princess Hannah grabbed their swords and raced to the old man, but when they reached him, their swords also vanished.

"You're Hal," said Edison. "You're hacking the universe. You're making things disappear."

"Now I know why everyone thinks you're such a talented detective. Good job, Edison." With that comment, Hal splashed another potion on Edison, and he was destroyed.

Edison spawned in his bed, but he looked down, and Puddles wasn't by his side. He called out for the ocelot, but Puddles didn't arrive. Edison wanted to get back to his friends. When he tried to TP to them, it didn't work.

"What's going on?" Edison questioned, even though there was nobody there to hear him.

Edison attempted to TP again. As he tried, he lost a heart in his health bar. Now if he even attempted to TP, he would be damaged and lose hearts. He was panicked. He worried about Hal's capabilities. Edison looked over at his potion stand. He wanted to brew more potions because he wanted to be prepared when he saw Hal. However, he realized he was still out of Nether wart, which was an essential ingredient.

"Edison!" Billy crashed through the door.

"What happened with Hal? Where are Anna and Princess Hannah?"

"It was awful." Billy caught his breath. "They all disappeared."

"What do you mean? He destroyed them?"

Billy replied, "No, he didn't destroy them, but he has special powers. He's a master hacker."

"What type of powers? Where are they?" asked Edison.

"I don't know, but I think they're in the dungeon with Princess Hannah's family."

"We have to find them," Edison said, then added, "I also can't find Puddles."

"Do you think Hal did something to the universe that removed the ocelots?" questioned Billy.

"I don't know, but we have to find out," said Edison.

The duo sprinted out of Edison's bungalow toward the desert. But they stopped when they heard someone say, "Where do you think you're going?"

7
ROBBED

Edison pulled a bottle of potion from his inventory, but like the diamond sword, it vanished before his eyes.

"What are you doing?" asked Edison.

"I have the power to take any item you own." Hal walked closer to Edison and pressed an enchanted diamond sword against his chest.

"Why are you doing this?" Billy screamed as he sprinted toward Hal with a wooden sword. When Billy reached Hal, the sword was no longer in hands.

Hal replied, "Why not?" and disappeared.

"I'm so glad he's gone." Edison let out a sigh of relief.

"But he stole our swords. I had only a diamond sword and a wooden one, and now I don't have any. What are we going to do? I can't battle Hal or anyone now. We have to go mining so I can craft another one." Billy said this all in one breath, and he was exhausted.

"I have only one sword left, or I'd lend you one. I do have a bunch of potions, but the only way we can fight him is if we surprise him," said Edison.

"How can we surprise him? We don't even know where he lives." Billy was very upset. "And I want to find Anna. I don't like the idea of her being trapped somewhere."

"And Princess Hannah," added Edison.

"Yes, we have to find them," Billy agreed. "And we have to stop Hal, but how?"

How? That was a question they had asked a lot. They were always trying to solve cases, and with each case, there was a point where they were left questioning how they could solve it. At this point the case seemed impossible, but Edison and Billy never walked away from a challenge.

"We have to find Hal!" declared Billy.

"But how? Where is he?" asked Edison.

Edison was shocked when he heard a voice call out, "I'm right here. I'm everywhere."

"Hal!" Billy screamed and lunged toward the gray-haired man, clutching his only bottle of potion from his inventory, but it vanished before he could throw it.

"You're not playing fair," Billy cried as Hal struck him with his diamond sword.

"Who said I had to play fair?" Hal asked as he sprinkled some potion of Invisibility on himself and disappeared.

Edison rushed to his friend's side. "Are you okay?" Edison grabbed some milk from his inventory and handed it to his friend.

Billy sipped the milk. "What is wrong with that guy?"

"I don't know, but we're going to stop him and find our friends." As Edison spoke, he eyed his brewing stand and noticed the large chest where he stored all of his potions was missing. He sprinted to the stand. "Billy, I think Hal stole all of my potions."

"How many do you have left in your inventory?"

Edison panicked when he counted the potions and realized he had only four bottles left. "Four."

"I don't have any. Before we stop Hal, we have to brew more potions," Billy said. "If we don't have a well-stocked inventory, we're just wasting time."

"I agree," Edison said. "But I don't have any Nether wart, and I need that to brew lots of potions. "

"We're going to have to go to the Nether. I have all the supplies to build a portal in my inventory." Billy walked out the door of the bungalow and began crafting a portal to the Nether.

"I'm not sure we should travel to the Nether now," Edison said. "We should go to the desert and save our friends."

"There's no point if we don't have any resources," protested Billy.

"But why should we bother brewing a bunch of potions if Hal has the ability to steal from us?"

"We can't even stage a surprise attack if we have no weapons," Billy rationalized.

"What about a bow and arrow? Or we can use command blocks to summon a Wither or an Ender Dragon, and he'd have to battle those mobs."

"And so would we," Billy dismissed Edison's strategies of attack.

"But the Nether? Now?"

"I think it's the only way we can save our friends. You know I'm a good treasure hunter, and I'll be able to gather all of the resources very quickly, right?"

"Yes, I know you're a great treasure hunter, but still it's a big trip." Edison realized there was no reason to protest. The portal was almost finished because Billy had been constructing it the entire time Edison was trying to come up with another plan.

"Just put on your armor," said Billy.

Edison pulled out his diamond armor and suited up. "I wish we didn't have to go to the Nether."

"I don't know any other way. We will go to the Nether and gather Nether wart and maybe some other ingredients, and then we'll head back. It won't take long, I promise."

Edison had made promises like that before. They were hard to keep, but they were always set with good intentions. However, Edison knew a trip to the Nether wasn't going to be quick. It would take time to find the Nether wart, and they'd have to fight fiery mobs. He quickly checked his inventory and counted the snowballs. He had enough snowballs and arrows to survive and gather the Nether wart, although he still reluctantly stood on the platform and watched as the purple mist surrounded them.

As they stood on the portal, Billy called out, "Edison, who is that?" Edison looked out through the purple mist and saw two men wearing blue baseball hats and sunglasses. They were identical. Billy screamed out to them as they entered Edison's bungalow.

"Stop! That's not your house. You can't go in there!" Billy's voice was loud, but the men didn't turn around.

"I have to stop them," said Edison, but it was too late. They were in the middle of the Nether, and a cluster of ghasts flew toward them.

Two fireballs shot at them, and Edison used his fist to deflect the ball that flew close to his unarmored body.

"What happened to my armor?" Edison screamed as he looked at his shirt. "I just had armor on."

"I know what happened," Hal called out as he charged toward them with a diamond sword. The two men with blue baseball caps and sunglasses trailed behind him.

8

NETHER START

"We're outnumbered," Edison whispered to Billy.

"Use your bow and arrow," Billy said as he pulled his bow from his inventory and shot an arrow at Hal. He was surprised the arrow struck Hal's arm and he cried out in pain. Billy thought the arrow would have disappeared midflight.

"You can't escape me." Hal was infuriated. He looked back at the identical guys behind him and ordered, "Go get them!"

The two men in blue baseball caps, who Edison assumed were Hal's makeshift hacker army, sprinted toward them, but before they reached Edison and Billy, they were struck by fireballs from the ghasts, and they lost hearts. Hal screamed at his minions, and Edison realized that Hal wasn't as organized as he appeared.

Edison used this opportunity to shoot an arrow at

Hal, which struck his other unarmored arm, and he yelled, "*Give me back my armor!*"

Edison knew if he didn't get his armor back, he'd never survive. He didn't have any diamonds, and it had taken him a very long time to gather all of the precious stones to craft the armor and the sword. Without good armor he would have a hard time surviving in the universe.

"I want my armor back!" Edison demanded again.

Billy was still wearing his armor and was worried it would disappear as he shot arrows at the two men in baseball hats. One of the men was already weakened from the ghost's fireball and was destroyed.

"You're going to pay for this," hollered Hal.

Edison shot an arrow at the other minion, destroying him, and screamed at Hal, "Your army is weak, and you're a thief. Give me back my armor."

"*Never!*" Hal screamed and disappeared.

"Thankfully, he's gone," Billy said as he kept an eye out for fiery mobs in the sky.

"But I have no armor. There is no way I'm going to survive, and I want to save our friends. What am I going to do?"

Billy remembered the chest Anna had in her home. It had extra armor and supplies, which she was always willing to lend people when they were in need. "How about going to Anna's and getting armor from her chest?"

"I guess so. I don't think she'd mind," said Edison. "And if I don't have my armor, I won't be able to save her."

"We just have to get the Nether wart, and then we can go to Verdant Valley. But if we don't get the Nether wart now, I don't have any more resources left in my inventory to construct another portal," explained Billy.

"Okay, but we have to find a Nether fortress," said Edison as they walked along a hot lava river. "We always seem to find Nether wart there."

Edison was upset that he didn't create a Nether wart farm. He had once met another alchemist who had a Nether wart farm, and he always thought it seemed like a great idea. As he told Billy about the Nether wart farm, Billy asked, "Why don't we ask that alchemist for Nether wart? The entire Overworld is in trouble, and we need to get all the help we can."

Edison hadn't seen this alchemist in a long time. His name was Julian, and Edison had met the other alchemist when he was low on potions for his stand. They did a trade so Edison would have enough potions for his customers. He knew Julian lived in a forest biome quite far from them, and he wasn't quite sure where Julian's town, Forest Haven, was located. He didn't want to travel to see Julian, but Billy was right: they needed help. They couldn't do this alone. This wasn't a simple case of finding someone or stopping a griefer. This was trying to stop the destruction of the Overworld. They were dealing with a master hacker. He wished he could find Andrew. Andrew had told them that he had been following Hal for a long time. Edison was sure Andrew knew a lot about Hal and probably knew his weaknesses.

Edison's mind was brought back to his current situation in the Nether when Billy climbed high atop a bridge over the lava river and called out, "I see a Nether fortress."

"Great!" Edison exclaimed and followed Billy toward the Nether fortress. Edison's heart raced as they approached the fortress. There were blazes on the ground, and the fiery beasts rose and readied for an attack when they spotted Edison and Billy. Without his armor, Edison felt incredibly vulnerable and worried that he would be destroyed before he could extract the Nether wart from the fortress. Usually Edison was excited when he saw a blaze. Even though it was a hard mob to destroy, you were rewarded with blaze rods. He used the blaze rods when crafting a brewing station.

One of the blazes shot a trio of potent fireballs at them. Edison jumped back to avoid the blast as he aimed his bow and arrow at the multi-limbed yellow mob that rose from the ground.

Billy aimed his arrow and destroyed a blaze. "Got it!" he called out and picked up the blaze rod, which he handed to his friend.

"Thanks!" Edison said as he watched his friend destroy the other blaze. He leaned over and picked up the blaze rod.

When the duo entered the Nether fortress, they heard a bouncing sound in the main room.

"Oh no," Edison said. "Magma cubes."

"That's not that hard to battle," Billy tried to remain positive, but he had to admit that he was worried about his friend Edison. You could only survive a limited time in the Nether without armor.

"I see Nether wart," Edison sprinted toward the staircase and gathered the Nether wart that grew on the side of the staircase next to a patch of soul sand.

"You get the Nether wart and soul sand," said Billy. "I will deal with the magma cubes."

Edison tried to pick the Nether wart as quickly as possible, because he wanted to help his friend, but as he pulled the Nether wart that grew in the Nether fortress, he felt a sharp pain in his back. He turned around and gasped when two wither skeletons stood inches from his unarmored body. His brown hair fell in his face and the wither skeleton's sword ripped his gray T-shirt. He had two hearts left. He pulled one of his last bottles of potion from his inventory and splashed the wither skeletons, but his potion didn't weaken the tough mob.

"Help!" Edison called out weakly, but his voice was low, and he knew Billy couldn't hear him. Edison was ready to surrender when Andrew stormed into the Nether fortress wearing diamond armor over his denim jacket and destroyed the two wither skeletons with his diamond sword. He picked up a dropped skull and bone.

"How did you find me?" asked Edison.

"I wasn't looking for you," replied Andrew.

9
THE CHEST

Billy exploded into the main room, declaring, "I destroyed the magma cubes."

"Good job," said Andrew.

"Andrew." Billy was shocked to see him in the Nether fortress. "Where are Anna and the Princess?"

"They're in the dungeon. I was with them too, but I was able to escape. I followed Hal to the Nether. I had no idea I'd find you guys here," he said.

"I'm glad you're here. Do you happen to have any extra armor?" asked Edison.

"No." Andrew looked at Edison's unarmored chest. "We have to get out of here. You aren't going to survive much longer without your armor. Also, I want us to find Hal. We have to stop him. He has something awful planned for the Overworld."

"What?" asked Billy.

"He is going to hack the entire universe. He is

47

going to steal everyone's goods and then he wants to put the universe on hardcore mode," Andrew explained as Edison gathered the last of the Nether wart.

"How do you know this?" asked Edison.

"I overheard him talking to his two followers," he said.

"I hope that he isn't far along with this plan," said Billy.

"Me too," Andrew said.

Edison finished gathering the Nether wart and said, "I'm ready to go."

Edison was surprised when he heard someone call out, "Where are you going?"

Edison looked down at the Nether wart that was in the palm of his hand. It was missing. He looked at his inventory, ready to grab a potion to throw at Hal, who stood in the center of the Nether fortress accompanied by his two minions, but as he reached into his inventory, he found it was empty.

Billy looked at his inventory, and it was also empty. Hal laughed as he saw their shocked expressions.

"You're no match for me," Hal announced, and he disappeared along with his two minions and Andrew.

"What happened?" asked Billy. He was still trying to process the situation.

"Hal is incredibly powerful. I have nothing in my inventory," said Edison as his eyes filled with tears.

"We have to get out of here." Billy sprinted out of the Nether fortress and toward the portal back to the Overworld. "We have to get to Anna's house and replenish our supplies."

As they stood on the portal, surrounded by purple mist, Edison said, "If Andrew is correct, this is going to be a very hard battle."

The duo emerged in Verdant Valley as a loud, thunderous boom shook the lush village. Two skeletons spawned inches from the duo as Billy said, "I hope he didn't put the universe on hardcore mode."

"Me too," Edison said as he sprinted from the bony beasts. He had no weapons to fight any mobs, and he didn't even have food to regain his energy.

Anna's house was nearby, and Edison and Billy rushed through the rain until they reached her front door. When they opened the door, they found Hal standing in the small living room. He looked down at the chest. "Is this what you're looking for?"

Edison and Billy stood silently. Hal spoke, "You don't have to say anything, because I know everything. I made Anna tell me everything she had stored in her house, and once she confessed that she had this chest, I knew you'd come looking for it. Well, I'm here to tell you that it's too late."

"Too late?" Edison asked. He took a deep breath. He worried that they were on hardcore mode. He also worried that Anna had been destroyed already. The universe could be over, and Edison was heartbroken.

"Yes," Hal clarified. "It's too late. You're all my prisoners now. We're off to the dungeon."

Edison was slightly relieved; he'd rather be a prisoner than destroyed. Although he'd admit he didn't like either option. He also was glad to be reunited with Anna, who he assumed was also still trapped in the dungeon. He hadn't seen her in a while, and he knew once they were reunited with her, they'd be able to come up with a plan to fight Hal.

Andrew still had a few potions and sword in his inventory. He splashed a potion on Hal and then sprinted toward him with his diamond sword, but Hal called for his two minions. The minions entered Anna's house and struck Andrew with their diamond swords, destroying him.

Edison hoped the universe wasn't on hardcore mode, and he hoped he'd see Andrew in the dungeon.

"You guys want to be next?" One of the minions called out to Edison and Billy. They stood silently.

Hal smiled. "They will happily go into the dungeon."

The rain was still falling, and Edison could hear the drops landing on the window. Thunder shook the small house. Zombies ripped the door from the hinges and reached for the minions. They were taken by surprise, and the zombies destroyed them. Hal wasn't prepared for their destruction and fumbled. He swung the diamond sword at the zombies, but he fell back and into a bunch of bottles of potion of Harming and was destroyed.

The instant Hal was destroyed, the sun came out. Edison rushed to the chest, which Hal accidently left in Anna's house, and looted the chest. They filled their inventories with the diamond swords and bottles of potion, quickly put on the diamond armor, and raced out of Anna's house.

As they sprinted from Anna's house, they heard their friends Erin and Peyton call to them. "Edison! Billy!"

Peyton asked, "Where have you been? Where's Anna?"

Erin's voice cracked when she asked, "What's going on? The Overworld seems to be in turmoil. We were hoping Anna knew what was going on."

"There is a master hacker trying to destroy the Overworld," said Edison, "but I don't have time to explain. Do you want to help us?"

"Of course," they replied in unison.

"Great," said Edison, "because we're going to need all the help we can get."

"Where are we going?" asked Erin, as they sprinted out of Verdant Valley.

"We have to go back to the desert. Anna is trapped in a desert dungeon," explained Billy.

Peyton and Erin shrieked in horror. Peyton said, "This is going to be tough."

"Do you have well-stocked inventories?" asked Edison.

Billy spotted Hal in the distance. "It doesn't matter what they have in their inventories, because we will lose everything soon."

"What are you talking about?" asked Erin.

"You'll see," Edison said as he watched Hal sprint toward them.

10

SWAMP TALES

"I have an idea," said Edison as he pulled a potion of Invisibility from his inventory and splashed it on himself and the others. "We have to take off our armor and put away our weapons," he told them. "Let's meet in the swamp biome. By the house we had crafted."

"I don't know where that is," said Peyton.

"Me either," Erin told him.

"It's on the shore. It's not a big biome, so you shouldn't have a problem finding it," Edison reassured them, and then set off for the swamp, bolting past Hal, who looked upset that they had vanished on their own.

The trip to the swamp biome was long. Edison reached the forest when the potion began to wear off and he was visible. At first he saw his legs, and soon his entire body was back to normal. He looked around for his friends. He assumed they would be close by and that the potions they took would be wearing off too, but he didn't see anyone. He looked in his newly stocked inventory and found a bottle of potion of Swiftness and took a gulp. He wanted to get to the swamp quickly, and the potion gave him the strength to make it to the swamp before the sun had set. As Edison approached the small house he had built with his friends, three bats flew through the sky, and he saw a full moon. Edison didn't want to repeat the last experience he had in the swamp biome. He didn't want to waste his energy battling slimes and witches. To ward off potential hostile mobs, Edison placed a torch on the side of the small house.

"Edison," a voice called out.

Edison looked up and saw Andrew walking toward him. Andrew smiled. "I was hoping I'd find you here. I stumbled upon this house before, and Anna had told me that you guys had built it."

"I'm so glad to see you," said Edison. "I thought Hal had put the universe on hardcore mode, and I was worried that you were destroyed."

"No," said Andrew. "He hasn't done that yet, but it's just a matter if time. We have to stop him. Let's go to the desert now. I'm sure he's waiting for us there. He definitely knows you want to save Anna and Princess Hannah and are going to showing up at the dungeon."

"That's our plan, but I have to wait for my friends." Edison explained that they had recruited two friends from their town and they would help them battle Hal.

"Great. The more people we have, the better. He is

a very skilled hacker," Andrew said as a bat flew close to his head. He looked at the bat fly past and remarked, "This isn't a good sign. I know once you see bats and a full moon, it's just a matter of time before you see a witch."

"You're right," Edison said as a witch scuttled down the path toward them. She clutched a bottle of potion. Andrew leaped at the witch and struck her with his diamond sword, but she was able to splash a potion on him. Andrew couldn't move—the potion weakened him to a point of immobility.

"Help!" Andrew cried, but his voice was faint.

Edison pulled some milk from his inventory and attempted to hand it to Andrew as Edison also raced to the witch. He slammed his diamond sword into the witch's purple-robed body with one hand, and with the other hand, he tossed the potion to Andrew, who gobbled it up and regained his strength. With renewed energy, Andrew sprinted toward the witch and obliterated her.

"Edison!" Billy called out.

Edison turned around and saw his friends sprinting toward him. He told them to meet inside the house. When the gang was in the small house by the swampy shore, Edison introduced Erin and Peyton to Andrew, and then he said, "We have to come up with a plan."

"Yes," Andrew agreed and explained, "We are dealing with a serious criminal. I have been following him for years."

"How did you meet him?" asked Erin.

Andrew finally told the story of how he met Hal. "I was a treasure hunter, and I was searching for treasure in End City. If you've ever been there, you know it's a very harsh biome that pays off with its rewards, but it is far from easy. I was on an End Ship when I had unearthed treasure after battling a shulker. When I was about to return home, I spotted a man with gray hair. I didn't say anything to him, but when I returned to the Overworld, my treasure from End City was missing."

"Hal stole your treasure?" asked Billy.

"That wouldn't have been that bad. I've been treasure hunting for years and have had tons of loot taken from me," replied Andrew.

"Then what happened?" asked Peyton.

"He found out where I lived and started to steal everything from me. When he was done taking all of my stuff, he robbed the rest of the people in the town, and no matter how hard we tried to hide our stuff, he'd find a way to take everything from our chests, and soon he had stolen from all the shops in the village. Eventually everyone moved away, and the town was left abandoned. I don't see anyone I used to know, and I have been wandering around the Overworld trying to spot Hal. In the time since I've been trailing him, he has gotten stronger. I also notice that when I run into him when I'm underwater, he doesn't have the same amount of power. He hasn't quite mastered hacking under the water."

"That's a really sad story. I hope once we defeat Hal, all of your friends can move back to your old town," said Erin.

"Yes, that's my dream. I want to travel around the Overworld to find all of the people who left and let them know it's safe to return to the town." Tears filled Andrew's eyes as he spoke.

"What was the name of the town?" asked Billy.

"Forest Haven." Andrew described the scenic town, and he went into great detail about his home.

Edison said, "I know someone from that town."

"Really?" Andrew asked.

"Yes, he's an alchemist."

"Julian?"

"Yes," said Edison. "He's an old friend."

"He was a friend of mine too, but I have no idea where he is today. Hal destroyed my town. I will never forgive him," said Andrew.

A bat flew past the window, and Edison could see the moon in the dark sky. "I think we should get some sleep. Tomorrow we're going to the desert, and we need our energy."

They said good night, and drifted off to a peaceful sleep, but were awoken when they heard a loud scream.

"Oh my!" Erin hollered.

"What?" asked Edison.

"All of my stuff is missing!" she screamed.

The rest of the gang checked their inventories, and they were all empty.

11

DUNGEON

There was no time to formulate a plan. Within seconds of discovering their inventories were emptied, Hal and his two minions stormed into the small swamp house.

Hal declared, "You're going to the dungeon."

They couldn't fight back—they had nothing—and they followed Hal and his evil soldiers to the desert. The walk through various biomes was silent and solemn. As they walked, Edison tried to think of plan to get away from Hal, but he knew it was pointless. The only positive aspect of this capture was being reunited with Anna. Anna was a great strategist, and he knew once they spoke, they'd be able to come up with a plan.

It was dusk as they approached the desert, which they could see through the leafy biome. With the desert in sight, Hal became more confident and said, "Welcome to the rest of your time in this universe. You will be in the dungeon when the Overworld comes to an end."

"You're so smart, boss," one of the minions smiled.

Edison didn't understand why anybody would want to destroy the Overworld. There was no reason to ruin other people's lives. He asked Hal, "Why would you want to ruin a world that people enjoy?"

"I'm a master hacker, and this is the ultimate challenge," Hal replied, as if destroying the entire Overworld was just another accomplishment like reaching a new level in a game.

"I'm sure there are other ways you can challenge yourself," Edison reasoned with Hal, but Hal didn't want to hear any of Edison's opinions. Hal took out his diamond sword, swung it at Edison and told him to be quiet. As Edison lost a heart, he spotted four skeletons spawning in the leaf-covered path in front of them, but he kept quiet and didn't warn Hal about the bony beasts. One of the skeletons shot an arrow that pierced Hal's arm. He turned around and yelled at Edison, "Why didn't you tell me there were skeletons?"

Edison didn't reply. Hal tried to battle the skeletons as Edison sidled up to his friends. "Let's have the skeletons destroy us." He spoke softly because he didn't want Hal and the minions, who were busy battling the skeletons, to hear his plan. "If we're destroyed, we can respawn in the swamp and escape."

Billy agreed this was a great plan, but before they could race in front of the arrows and lose hearts, Hal had destroyed the bony beasts. Hal yelled at them, "We have to hurry to the dungeon. We need to get there before nightfall."

He handed each of them a bottle of potion of Swiftness and forced them to drink it and sprint as fast as they could to the desert. They raced past cacti and up sand dunes in the dark until Hal stopped in front of a patch of ground and ordered them to stop, "Don't move and don't talk."

Hal leaned down and lifted a grate that was camouflaged into the ground and told them to climb down a ladder that went deep underneath the sandstone ground.

Muffled voices could be heard, but Edison wasn't sure which direction they were coming from. The ladder was very long, and Edison felt like he was climbing down the ladder forever. When he finally reached the bottom of the ladder, he heard a familiar voice that made him happy.

"Edison," Anna called out.

Edison looked over and saw Anna, Princess Hannah, and Hannah's family on the other side of a gate. Edison said, "Anna, I'm happy to see you, but not under these circumstances."

Anna stared at Edison and smirked. He knew that look. It was the one Anna made when she had a good idea, and Edison felt confident they'd be able to escape from this dungeon. They had to escape and stop Hal from destroying the universe. He also wanted Hal to stop the glitch that removed the ocelots. He missed Puddles.

Hal was the last person to climb down the stairs, and he took out a key and opened the gate. "Get in here," he shouted at them.

The gang walked silently into the jail that Hal had created in this dungeon. Inside the sandy jail was an empty chest. Edison looked in the chest and wondered why Hal had left an empty chest. Was he trying to torment them? Edison decided not to ask any questions. He just listened to what Hal had to say.

When they were all locked inside the jail, Hal began to speak. "Since I have taken all of your resources and emptied your inventories"—he giggled as he said this—"I will provide you with just enough food to survive. I wouldn't want any of you being destroyed because you have a diminished health bar. So I will fill up this chest with food, and you can distribute it amongst yourselves."

Edison stared at the chest as it filled with various foods, from cakes to chicken. The chest had enough food for a large feast. He couldn't believe this was the food ration for the day. He realized Hal wanted them to stay alive, and as he eyed the food he came up with a plan. He looked over at Anna, and her smirk grew wider. Edison realized Anna had come up with the same plan.

Hal and his minions climbed up the ladder, and the gang could hear the grate being placed atop the ground. They were trapped.

Billy grabbed an apple from the chest.

"Don't eat it," Anna called out.

"Why not?" Billy questioned. "I'm very hungry."

"I know, but I have plan," said Anna.

"What is it? Starve us?" questioned Billy.

"Yes," Anna and Edison said in unison.

"What are you talking about?" Billy was confused.

"If we don't eat, we will be destroyed and respawn out of here. Hal hasn't noticed that our health bars are very low. If I don't eat today, I will probably be destroyed by tomorrow. Look at your health bars. You guys have been traveling and not eating, right?"

Billy looked at his health bar. "Yes, my health bar is also very low."

"Yes, we have to stop eating, and then we can come up with a plan. I think if we get out of here, we can defeat Hal," said Anna.

Erin loved the plan, but she also wanted Anna to know about Hal's tricks. Hal was capable of emptying inventories, and he was leaving everyone in the Overworld without any way to defend each other.

"He looted my chest, right?" asked Anna.

"Yes," Edison said.

Peyton had a plan. "If we find out where he lives, I bet we'll find everybody's stuff."

Prince Elias said, "I know where Hal lives."

"Tell us," said Edison.

12

HACKER ARMY

Prince Elias told them about a big underwater treasure hunt he had taken. "I saw a large ocean monument where he stored all of his treasures. It seems as if this is the only biome where he can't hack, and maybe he knows others can't either, so he believes his treasures are safe underwater."

Andrew confirmed this. "Yes, I told you that we all had to stock up on potions of Water Breathing."

Edison realized that he still needed pufferfish, and then remembered that he had nothing. Hal had stolen all of his potions and his ingredients. In fact, Hal had stolen everything. He didn't have any way of traveling underneath the water. "How can we go under the water? We don't have a potions for breathing under water."

Edison disliked poking holes in people's plans, but he also knew a good detective had to challenge the people around him or they'd never solve the case.

"That's true. Do you think he has a place where he stored his looted treasure in the Overworld?" asked the queen.

Andrew paced the length of the small cell. "I have been following him for a very long time, and I haven't come across any storage facilities for his loot."

Prince Elias said, "I bet it's somewhere over here."

"What?" asked Peyton.

The Prince explained, "When I encountered him in the desert and questioned him, he became very aggressive and trapped us down here."

Andrew interrupted, "Yes, you're right, he's never done anything like that, which must mean we are close to discovering something."

Edison agreed. He did believe Hal felt threatened by them, and he wanted to stop them from investigating and stopping him. "We have to find out where he's hiding his treasure."

Peyton's stomach rumbled, and she excused herself. The group was famished, and it was hard to stare at the chest filled with food without taking something. She eyed the cookies and reached for one.

"Stop!" Erin screamed.

"What are you doing?" asked Anna. "We had a plan."

The shouting must have alerted the minions that something was brewing in the prison, and they opened the hatch and walked down the seemingly never-ending ladder until they stood outside the prison gate.

"What's going on here?" asked one of the men.

"Nothing," said Anna. "We were just having a disagreement on who gets what from the chest. We're all very hungry, and we each want certain foods."

"Okay," the minion said. "Just keep it down."

The two minions climbed up the ladder, and when the grate was closed, the gang began to whisper.

The king said, "We have to be very quiet down here. I only have a few minutes before I am destroyed due to my health bar, and I want to be able to respawn in the desert temple. I will try to find out where Hal is hiding all of his resources."

Andrew, who was minutes away from being destroyed, agreed this was the best plan. When he was destroyed, he'd search for the Hal's loot.

"We have to come up with a plan after we are destroyed," said Edison. "We can't fight Hal if we separate. We aren't strong enough. We need to stick together to battle him."

"Yes," said Anna. "Should we find a place to meet after we respawn?"

"Let's meet in Farmer's Bay," said Edison. "It's on the shore, so we have access to the underwater world. Also we have friends there who can help us."

"That's a great idea," said the king, but the second he uttered those words, his health bar diminished, and he was destroyed.

"Dad!" Princess Hannah screamed.

"Don't scream," Andrew whispered. "You don't want Hal's bullies to come down here and attack us."

Princess Hannah was upset. Despite being in the

dungeon prison, she was happy to be finally reunited with her father, and now he was gone. However, she knew he'd respawn in their home, and he'd be able to help them find Hal's loot. As tears filled her eyes, she watched her mother and then her brother disappear. Tears streamed down her cheeks, and her stomach rumbled. She was incredibly hungry. She eyed the chest again and reached for an apple.

"You can't eat an apple," Peyton said. "Your health bar is so low. If you just hold out for a little while longer, you will be destroyed."

She had a very low health bar, but she couldn't wait any longer. She needed an apple. Her stomach was empty. She was in pain. Also, when she respawned she wouldn't have any food. Princess Hannah could envision how juicy the apple would taste and how it would fill her painfully empty stomach. "I'm sorry," she said as she grabbed the apple and opened her mouth to take a bite. "I can't starve myself. I am so hungry. I can't even—"

Princess Hannah's health bar emptied as she spoke. Edison said, "Wow, I hope she's okay when she respawns. She was starving."

Billy reminded him, "The entire Overworld will starve if we don't stop Hal. Also, if he starves us and puts the universe on hardcore mode, we will never respawn."

"We have to stop him," said Andrew.

Sounds of footsteps were heard in the distance.

"What is that?" asked Edison.

Billy looked up and said in a hushed voice, "I think they are coming down here."

"Now we're in trouble," Edison sighed.

"What are we going to do?" asked Peyton.

"He's going to see they're missing, and he'll punish us. What happens if he puts us on hardcore mode?" Erin questioned as her voice shook.

The gang could hear the minions remove the gate from the sandy desert ground and climb down the ladder. The minions arrived in front of the prison cell and screamed, "What?"

"We can explain," said Edison.

"You better!" said one of Hal's minions.

Billy and the gang looked at Edison, eager to see what he'd say and how he'd "explain" what had happened. None of them had any clue how they'd describe how a bunch of the prisoners had gone missing.

Edison said, "You gave us the food too late. They were starving. Their health bars were very low, and Princess Hannah was destroyed before she could even take a bite out of the apple. If you treated them better, they would have lasted a lot longer."

Anna knew her health bar was about to go empty, and she reached for a cookie. She opened her mouth to take a bite, and she disappeared.

"Oh no!" cried one of the minions. "Hal's going to kill us."

It was at that moment Edison came up with a master plan.

13

FOOL OR FRIEND

"You guys better eat this food," ordered the minions. "You can't let your health bars get that low."

Edison picked up a cookie and ate it. "Of course, we want to remain strong. We wouldn't want to get you in trouble."

"Who said we were in trouble?" one of the minions shouted.

"You seemed very upset when you saw Princess Hannah and her family were missing," said Edison.

"Yes," a minion replied, and it didn't matter which one because they both seemed to think alike.

The other one added, "Our job was to make sure you guys were still down here, and we wanted to do a good job."

Edison smiled. "I think you're doing a good job. This cookie tastes very good."

"Thank you," a minion replied.

"What are your names?" asked Andrew.

He understood Edison's plan. He was trying to befriend the minions in hopes that they would turn against Hal.

One of the minions replied, "Ron."

The other said, "Don."

"Well, Ron and Don," said Peyton, "it's nice to meet you. I'm Peyton, and these are my friends." She introduced Ron and Don to Erin, Billy, Andrew, and Edison.

"I know who you guys are," said Don.

"I'm sure you do. I just thought it was nice to have a formal introduction," explained Peyton.

"Just eat your food," said Ron.

She picked up a piece of cake and ate it. "This is the best piece of cake I've ever eaten. Thank you."

"You're welcome," said Don.

Ron watched Peyton eat the cake and said, "You guys had the food for a while. Why did it take you so long to eat it? If the others had eaten earlier, they might have survived down here."

"We were trying to divide it, and everyone wanted the same food. While we were figuring it out people's health bars grew lower, and before they could eat, they were destroyed," explained Billy.

Ron nodded. "I wonder if you did that on purpose?"

"Why would anyone do something like that on purpose?" asked Erin.

"You guys want to trick us," said Don.

"Trick you? You were the ones who bothered us. We were just living our simple lives in the Overworld when Hal came and ruined everything. I think it's funny that you are trying to make us the bad guys when you are the ones who are trying to trick everyone," Edison's voice grew louder as he spoke.

Ron asked if he would lower his voice. "I don't want Hal coming down here right now."

"Why? Are you worried you'll get in trouble?" asked Billy.

"I told you, we aren't in trouble, you're the ones who are in trouble," said Don.

"No," explained Erin. "The Overworld is in trouble, and you're the ones who are responsible for its impending destruction."

"Us?" questioned Ron.

"Yes. You're working with a man who has stolen from everyone. He took all of our resources from our inventory," said Erin.

"He also trapped us in a jail," added Peyton. "Does that sound like someone who is nice?"

"Hal isn't trying to be nice." Don laughed. "Now eat something or your health bar will get smaller."

Peyton picked up a cookie and took a bite. "Why do you work with Hal? He's so bad."

"And he's very destructive," said Erin.

"Hal is a genius," replied Ron.

Don explained, "He has a great plan for the Overworld. He's going to—"

Hal interrupted Don, as Hal rushed down the

ladder and screamed at him, "You aren't supposed to tell anyone about my plan."

"I'm sorry. I wasn't going to go into any details. I promise," said Don.

Hal looked in the prison. "There are people missing!"

"I know," Ron said. "I can explain."

"You better," said Hal.

"You didn't give them enough food. By the time they could eat, they were destroyed," said Ron.

"That's impossible. They were deliberately not eating in order to be destroyed. They want to spawn in their homes so they could help defeat me. Well, it's not going to work. Don and Ron, you better go find the others and bring them back here. I will deal with the ones that were left behind," Hal said.

Ron and Don sprinted up the ladder as Hal glared at the guys in the jail. "You are going to pay for this."

14

IN THE CHEST

Edison didn't know how they were going to get out of the jail. He had no plans, and he stared at Hal.

"What are you going to do to us?" asked Billy.

"You think you're so smart and you can defeat me, but you can't. I will find your friends, and they will be back here with you. Now I want to see you guys eat until your health bars are full. You are not getting out of here," hollered Hal.

The gang gorged themselves on the food in the chest. They ate apples, bread, cookies, and cake.

"I'm full," said Peyton.

"Your health bar isn't full yet. You have to keep eating," ordered Hal.

As Edison bit into an apple, he could see two skeletons spawn in the dimly lit dungeon. They stood behind Hal and pointed their arrows at him. He tried not to stare. He didn't want Hal to turn around and battle the bony beasts. Instead, Edison dropped the apple on the floor.

"What are you doing?" screamed Hal. "You have to eat that apple."

Hal was so distracted by Edison's antics that he barely noticed when two arrows pierced his unarmored skin. He didn't notice until his back radiated with pain and he screamed in agony. His hearts were diminishing, and his health bar was very low. He turned around to battle the bony beasts as two more spawned in the dungeon.

He pulled his armor from his inventory, but it was too late. Hal had lost too many hearts and was destroyed. The skeletons spotted the gang behind the bars and started shooting arrows at them.

"Put food in your inventories," Edison told his friends. They had to respawn with food to regain their health.

Normally when he saw skeletons, he either hid or got ready to battle, but now he was going to let the arrows pierce his body until he was destroyed. Instinctively he ducked when he saw the arrows fly toward him, but he knew this was a way out and made himself stand tall. At first, he winced when the first arrow ripped into his weak unarmored body, but then he thought about being released from this desert dungeon.

"Ouch!" Peyton cried as she was destroyed.

Erin covered her eyes when her friend was destroyed. Andrew did the same.

The pain of being destroyed never felt as good as

it did at that moment. Edison knew that once enough arrows hit him, he'd respawn in the swamp house. He also knew that Hal would come looking for them in the swamp house, and they'd have to make their escape quickly. He looked over at Billy, who was struck by numerous arrows, but still hadn't been destroyed.

Edison remembered the final arrow hitting his arm and waking up in a bed in the swamp house. Billy stared at him as he opened his eyes.

"I thought Peyton and Erin were destroyed before us," said Billy.

"They were," confirmed Edison.

"But they're not here," Billy pointed to the beds.

"I thought you were still in the dungeon," said Edison. "You were there when I was destroyed."

"We must have been destroyed at the same time," said Billy.

"Maybe Erin and Peyton left for Farmer's Bay. That's where we supposed to meet," suggested Edison, "and we have to get out of here. This is the first place Hal is going to look for us."

The duo sprinted from the house as Edison peered up at the sky. It was dusk, and the full moon was becoming visible in the evening. Edison and Billy picked up the pace because they didn't want to be attacked by a witch. Their inventories contained only food, not any other resources, which left them incredibly vulnerable to hostile mobs.

The trip to Farmer's Bay was long, and Billy expressed concern about traveling at night.

"We might not make it to Farmer's Bay since it's night time. I worry that we will be destroyed by hostile mobs. Maybe we should try and TP there," said Billy.

Edison spotted an opening in a cave. "I know this sounds nutty, but should we try and mine?"

"How?" asked Billy. "We don't have a pickaxe. Should we dig into the ground with our hands?"

Edison knew the idea wasn't well conceived, but he had no idea how else they would get their hands on minerals to trade for or craft a new armor.

The sky grew darker, creating an environment ripe for hostile mobs. Two skeletons spawned in the distance. They clutched their bows and aimed arrows at Edison and Billy.

"What are we going to do?" Billy brushed his hair from his face. "We're doomed."

Edison ordered, "Go into the cave!"

"But what about spiders?" asked Billy.

Edison didn't listen to a response. He was already deep in the cave. He tried to ignore the pair of red eyes glaring at him from the corner. Billy rushed into the cave and spotted the spider. "I told you this was a bad idea."

Edison sprinted deeper into the cave, trying to move farther from the spider when he tripped on a chest.

"Ouch!" His leg was skinned, and he'd ripped his gray shirt.

"Are you okay?" Billy called out as he sprinted toward his injured friend.

"Oh my!" exclaimed Edison.

"What happened?" asked Billy, but he didn't need a response. In the dark cave, he could make out the outline of a chest. "Is that a chest?" he asked.

Edison wished he had a torch. He needed light to properly inspect the floor of the cave, but even without a torch he could see three chests in front of him. He leaned down and opened one of the chests. Edison gasped when he saw the chest teeming with diamonds.

Edison grabbed the diamonds by the handful and placed them in his inventory as Billy opened the second chest, which was filled with emeralds. "You take the diamonds, and I'll grab the emeralds," said Billy.

"We have to open the third chest," said Edison.

Edison looked down the dark, narrow hallway in the cave. "I see more chests and a door."

"Do you think it's a stronghold?" asked Billy.

"I don't know, but we have to craft armor and swords out of these diamonds before we start exploring," said Edison.

Billy opened the next chest, which was filled with potions of Water Breathing. Edison opened the chest that was a few feet away from the original three chests, and it also contained potions of Water Breathing.

"We're going to need those for everyone," said Billy as he sprinted toward Edison and filled his inventory with the potions.

"These potions are going to come in very handy," said Edison.

"But we still need a crafting table," said Billy. "This

is all meaningless if we can't craft armor and a diamond sword. We need something to defend ourselves."

"True," Edison agreed, "but this is better than nothing. We have to take all of these bottles." Edison placed the final bottle of potion of Water Breathing in his inventory.

"Great." Billy looked at his inventory filled with emeralds and potions. Although they still needed a crafting table, they had scored some pretty good loot.

"We have to watch out for hostile mobs," warned Edison. "This cave is very dark, and it's the type of place where they spawn. Also, we have no idea what might spawn in the stronghold and make their way here."

Billy looked at the ground, inspecting the area for silverfish, but he didn't see any slimy bugs.

"I wonder if there are any more chests," said Billy as he looked at the ground in the cave while trying to avoid an attack from a cave spider. He searched for more chests in the dark cave and finally exclaimed, "I found more!"

"This is our lucky day," said Edison.

"It is!" a voice called out from the cave's entrance.

15

GHOST TOWN

Again, Edison instinctively went to reach for his sword, but it wasn't there. He had no way to defend himself against the person who entered the cave.

"Who's there?" Billy bravely called out.

There was no response. They could hear the rush of footsteps as the person rushed toward them.

Billy and Edison bolted deeper into the cave to avoid the seemingly unavoidable attack. Edison reached for the door to the stronghold when the voice called out again.

"Where are you going?"

Edison recognized the sound of the voice. He sprinted back toward the chests, where he saw Andrew dressed in his denim jacket.

"I see you found my fortune." Andrew pointed to the chests. "Normally I'd be furious with someone who stole from me, but given the current circumstances, I'm glad you guys were the first to find this stuff. I wasn't even sure it would still be here."

"We found diamonds and emeralds," said Edison.

"We need a crafting table," said Billy.

"I know," said Andrew. "If we had one, we could replenish our inventories."

"Where can we find one?" asked Edison.

"Forest Haven, the town that I lived in, wasn't far from here. If we return there, we can use the crafting table in my house. I left it there," said Andrew.

"Okay," said Billy. "Let's go.

Andrew said, "We can't go now. It's pitch dark out. We will be destroyed in a minute. We're going to have to stay here until it gets light out. We also have to hope that no hostile mobs spawn here."

Billy laughed. "I forgot that it was night time."

Edison looked at the ground. "Are there more chests in here?"

"Yes," said Andrew. "We should open them. I know I have a few chests with potions that we could use to defend ourselves."

Billy pulled some potions of Water Breathing from his inventory. "Do you want these back? We took them all."

"Because you wanted to have everyone use them, right?" asked Andrew.

"Yes," replied Billy.

"You can hold on to them. You can distribute them when we reach the shores of Farmer's Bay. I want everyone there when we find Hal under the water. I believe that's the only way we can stop him. He isn't as strong under there."

The trio looked through the chests scattered across the floor of the cave. They found two chests filled with potions of Weakness and another filled with potions that could weaken and harm.

"We can finally defend ourselves," said Edison.

"And you'll need to!" A deep voice boomed through the cave.

The trio stood up and saw Hal sprinting toward them. The older man with gray hair was inches from them when they doused him with every potion they could hold in their hands. But they only weakened him; they didn't destroy him.

Hal pulled a potion from his inventory, but as he grabbed it, the trio was able to spray Hal with a second barrage of potion, and he vanished.

"We have to get out of here," said Edison.

"But it's night," Billy reminded him.

"Edison's right, we have to get out of here," said Andrew. "We have no choice."

The gang sprinted out of the cave. Edison wished Andrew had a potion of Invisibility in one of the chests they had emptied, but as he raced through the dark night, he reminded himself that they were lucky to have filled their inventories with all of the loot. They were even luckier that Hal hadn't hacked their inventories and stolen all of their treasures.

"The town isn't far from here," Andrew reassured them.

It was dark out, and the gang kept a close eye out for hostile mobs, and they noticed two zombies lumbering toward them. The smell from the undead mob was nauseating, and they held their noses. Edison pulled potion from his inventory and sprinted toward the undead beasts and splashed them with potion. The vacant-eyed mobs were weakened when Billy and Andrew raced toward them with their potions. The undead beasts were destroyed. The gang spotted a few more zombies in the distance, and they armed themselves with potions as they raced toward the foul-smelling creatures of the night.

They were inches from the zombies when the sun came out. Their eyes were blinded by the sunlight, and they closed their eyes. When Edison finally opened his eyes and stopped squinting, he saw the forest was right in front of them. Large spruce trees that reached the sky were in sight.

"It's Forest Haven," exclaimed Andrew. He sprinted toward the biome that was thick with leaves. "You have to stay close behind me or I'll lose you. It's very easy to get lost in my biome," he explained. "But my house isn't far from here."

Edison and Billy followed closely behind Andrew, who led them down a path that was covered in leaves. The green leaves brushed against Edison's face as he made his way toward the town. When they reached the other side of the leaves, Edison saw a bunch of homes.

They sprinted past a small village, which was abandoned. The blacksmith's shop, the library, and the streets were emptied of people. The ghost town depressed Edison. He disliked seeing the town, which he assumed was once bustling, emptied. As he jogged through Forest Haven, he understood the devastating impact Hal had on the universe. Edison wasn't going to let him destroy Farmer's Bay or any other town in the universe.

"There's my house," said Andrew, pointing to a small wooden home next to a large tree.

Andrew slipped inside, and Edison and Billy followed him. Tears filled Andrew's eyes as he looked around the small wooden house. "This place looks exactly the same."

He stood by the crafting table, and Edison pulled diamonds from his inventory and handed them to Andrew. Andrew carefully crafted a diamond sword. "If we craft armor, I think we have enough diamonds to craft some for all of our friends. I think we actually have just enough for three swords."

"I wish we had enough for all of our friends, but that's better than nothing," said Billy.

"We can give them the potions that we have so they will have something to help them defend themselves."

A voice called out from the doorway, "Is someone there?" The voice was weak, and it jarred the gang. This was a ghost town, and they weren't expecting to see anybody in Forest Haven.

"Hello?" it called out again.

Edison and Andrew said in unison, "Julian?"

"Yes," he replied as he walked in with a cane.

"What happened to you?" asked Andrew, looking up from the crafting table.

"I was injured a while ago, and I returned home. I have been hiding in town. Hal doesn't think anybody is here, so he hasn't returned."

"We're trying to battle Hal," explained Billy.

"Good," said Julian. "He needs to be stopped."

Andrew crafted the first sword and handed it to Edison. "What do you think?"

It had been a long time since Edison held a sword, and it felt good to have the ability to fight back in battle. "This is perfect. Thank you."

Andrew crafted the next sword and handed it to Billy, who also thanked him. As Andrew worked on the final sword, Julian asked, "Where are you planning on battling Hal?"

"We're going to try and find him under water," said Billy.

"If you want, I have a lot of potion of Water Breathing. I have been saving it for a moment like this. Honestly, I never thought this moment would come, and I'd love to give you all of the potions I have in my house."

"We do have a lot of potion of Water Breathing," said Edison.

Andrew finished the final sword, which he placed in his inventory before he began to craft the armor. "I think we should take the additional bottles," he said. Then he asked Julian, "Unless you want to come with us?"

"I thought you'd never ask," he said. "I'd love to join you." He walked back home to gather the potions and met them outside of Andrew's house. They were suited up in armor and clutched their swords. Julian was also wearing diamond armor.

"How'd you keep the armor?" asked Andrew.

"I have my ways," Julian replied.

The gang sprinted out of Forest Haven toward Farmer's Bay. Julian trailed behind them with his cane. When they reached Verdant Valley, a loud, thunderous boom shook the ground, and rain created puddles on the ground.

"Hostile mobs are going to spawn," warned Andrew. "We don't want to use all of our resources, or we will be in trouble."

"But we have to get to Farmer's Bay. We're so close," said Edison.

Three skeletons spawned in the damp day and shot arrows at the group. The rainy arrows hit their armor and bounced off. Edison loved having armor again. It was so much easier to battle. As he raced toward the skeletons and leaped at them with his diamond sword, he could hear familiar voices call out in the distance.

Through the rain, Edison could see Anna's purple hair and red shirt, and he could hear her screaming, "Help!"

She wasn't battling skeletons: she was being destroyed by Hal.

16

UNDERWATER SEARCH

A skeleton's arrow pierced Edison's arm as he sprinted toward Anna and Hal. As he reached Anna, she had only one heart left, and Edison quickly tossed a potion on Hal that weakened him, and then sliced into his unarmored belly with his diamond sword. Now Hal had only one heart left.

As Edison delivered the final blow and destroyed Hal, Edison said, "You thought you were so powerful that you didn't need armor, but you were wrong."

Hal looked at Edison and said, "You'll pay for this." Then he was destroyed.

Although Hal had been destroyed for the moment, Anna was still incredibly vulnerable. Her purple hair was wet and stuck to her face, and her red plaid shirt was drenched. "When is this going to end?" she asked Edison. Her voice was weak, and she was exhausted.

"Take this." He handed Anna a bunch of bottles of

harming and some that she could drink to regain her strength. "This should help you. I promise you, we will get this to stop. We always do."

"You're so confident," Anna said as she drank a potion of Strength. She was about to splash a potion of Harming on a skeleton when the rain stopped and the sun came out.

"I told you it would get better." Edison smiled.

Andrew rushed over to Edison. "We have to get underneath the water now. We don't have a lot of time. He's going to come back."

Billy saw Petyon, Erin, Princess Hannah, and her family on the shores of Farmer's Bay. He handed them bottles of potion of Water Breathing. They all thanked him and took a big gulp, and then they collectively plunged into the deep blue sea.

A guardian swam past them, and the spiky fish wagged its tail, readying itself for an attack. The fish locked eyes with Billy, and he was caught in the fish's laser that quickly changed from purple to yellow. Billy's armor protected him from the serious impact, but he still lost two hearts.

"We have to get inside this ocean monument," Andrew said as he swam toward the ocean monument below them. It was being guarded by an elder guardian that was in the middle of a battle with a player that had swum into the monument before they arrived.

"Is that Hal?" asked Edison as he swam next to Andrew.

"No," Andrew said. "That's Ron."

"Or Don?" asked Billy.

"It's both of them." Andrew took a closer look. The elder guardian was in the midst of a battle with two people.

"We have to wait here," said Andrew.

Everyone swam next to Andrew, waiting for the destruction of the elder guardian. They tried to hide from Ron and Don as they watched the duo try to defeat the elder guardian, but they were having a hard time. They had both been struck with the Wither effect multiple times.

"They aren't very good fighters," said Princess Hannah.

"I know. We should help them, but it's sort of fun to watch," said Andrew.

"What happens if they attack us when we help them?" questioned Prince Elias.

"There's only one way we can find out, and we have to get into the ocean monument," said Andrew as he swam toward them. But he stopped when he saw Ron defeat the elder guardian and swim to pick up the prismarine drop. Andrew kept his distance to make sure Ron and Don didn't see him. The others watched Andrew as he swam at a slow pace toward the entrance.

Andrew waved to the others. He wanted them to follow him into the ocean monument. They swam into the grand prismarine ocean monument lit with sea lanterns, past a large room, and down a hall with a series of rooms. Andrew swam into the first room, a massive room with a roof comprised of sponges. "This isn't it."

he told them, and he swam toward the next room. As the gang got closer to the next room, they could hear voices.

"We found it. Great, we have to put all of this in our inventory," said Ron.

"I can't believe it," said Don. "We actually found it."

"We have to work fast. We don't want him finding out," said Ron.

Andrew peeked his head in the room. It was filled with gold bars, but behind the gold bars were numerous chests; Andrew couldn't even count how many chests were in the room.

"Guys." He looked at his new friends. "It looks like we found it," Andrew told them.

"Is Hal in there?" asked Anna.

"No," he explained. "Ron and Don are looting the room."

"Now I know why they were sticking with him," said Anna. "They were plotting to steal from him. "

They didn't have time to discuss the betrayal in Hal's world because as they floated by the room's entrance, they saw Hal spawn in the center of Ron and Don.

Hal screamed, "What are you doing?"

Ron and Don didn't respond with words. Instead they both took out their diamond swords and swam toward Hal. Ron ripped into Hal's arms with his diamond sword, and Don sliced into his legs. They were trying to hit any unarmored part of his body. Hal was losing hearts, but he wasn't destroyed. He fought back and swung his sword at Ron, cutting his shoulder.

"Why are you doing this? This is my treasure!" Hal shouted.

"Not anymore," said Don as he pounded the sword against Hal's legs.

"You were supposed to be my assistants. Why are you betraying me?" Hal asked as he struck Ron with his sword.

The gang just stayed by the entrance and watched. They couldn't believe their luck. They got to watch Hal's own people bring him down. Most of them were content watching the battle unfold, but Edison felt they should get involved.

"We don't want Ron and Don destroying Hal. If they do, we will have no idea where he'll respawn, and we want to capture him," said Edison.

"Can't we just watch them destroy each other?" asked Petyon.

"No," said Edison. "This is our perfect opportunity to capture Hal, and we have to do it now." Edison swam into the thick of the battle between Hal and Ron and Don.

"Edison," Hal called out. "Help me!"

"Help you?" Edison laughed. "I'm not here to help you."

"Why are you here?" Hal asked weakly.

"To capture you," said Edison.

Hal watched as the entire gang he had held prisoner in the desert dungeon swam into the room.

Ron and Don let out a collective gasp. "You're not taking us," said Ron.

Billy swam toward Ron and Don. Their hearts were low, and he grabbed them. "You're coming back to Farmer's Bay. All of you are going to be punished for trying to destroy the Overworld."

Edison held Hal. "You have to stop hacking and stealing from the Overworld."

"And destroying towns," said Julian. "You wiped Forest Haven from the map. It's a ghost town."

"You have to stop removing ocelots from the Overworld. I don't want to lose Scooter again," added Princess Hannah.

Hal was overwhelmed. All of these complaints about him swam around in his head. The strikes from Ron and Don's swords had weakened him, and he only had one heart left. He didn't even have enough energy to pull a potion of Invisibility from his inventory and splash it on himself and escape, which was his usual move.

"You're coming with us," said Anna. "All of you."

The trio had no choice. They had to swim back to the shore of Farmer's Bay with the gang. When they reached the shore, they walked toward the village. They brought Hal and his minions into the town hall. Edison pulled apples from his inventory and ordered them to eat. They had very low health bars, and he didn't want them getting destroyed as he interrogated them.

As the trio ate their apples, Edison and the gang pounded them with questions.

"How are you hacking? Is all of the stuff you stole from the folks in the Overworld in the ocean monument? How can you stop hacking? Were you using command blocks?"

Hal listened to all of the questions, but only replied, "I'm not answering anything."

17

MESSAGES

"**W**ell you don't have to tell us," said Anna. "We are going to put you in jail in Verdant Valley. Maybe one day, you'll change your mind and want to tell us, but for now you can just sit there and think about all of the bad things you did to the Overworld."

The trio didn't respond. Edison ordered them to empty their inventories. Hal pulled out a sword and a few potions from his inventory, and Ron and Don did the same.

"Show us your inventories. We want to make sure they are empty," ordered Billy.

The trio showed them their empty inventories, and the group carefully inspected them. They didn't want Hal, Ron, or Don having anything in the jail. They could use these items to escape and create more havoc on the Overworld.

The gang walked the criminals to the jail in Verdant Valley. Although the walk was silent, when they placed the trio in the small prison bedrock jail, the trio had an explosive fight. Anyone walking past the structure could hear the shouting.

"I can't believe you guys were stealing from me! You are the reason I was caught," Hal screamed.

"Us?" Ron and Don screamed back.

"Yes, if we were working together, they couldn't have caught us," screamed Hal.

Edison stood outside the jail. They couldn't see him, but he was keeping track of everything that they were shouting at each other. He knew that this was better than a confession, that if they kept shouting, they would eventually reveal something they didn't want Edison and the gang to know. They were very emotional and weren't thinking about what they were saying.

"We listened to you for such a long time, and we knew you would have just destroyed us once you had stolen everything from the Overworld," declared Don.

"I wasn't going to do that," Hal defended himself.

"Don't lie to us," said Ron. "We know what you had planned."

"But we were working together as a team," said Hal.

"We were never a team," screamed Don. "You were just using us to get whatever you wanted done. We saw you do this to others. You just put them on hardcore mode and destroy them when you're through. You are awful."

"But I wouldn't have done that to you. I wanted you to be with me when I gathered all of the treasure in the Overworld and lived a life under the water."

"Hal, how can we believe you?" asked Don.

"I taught you guys how to hack. I never did that with the others. I told you how to use the command blocks. I even brought you to the room behind the dungeon prison where I keep them."

Edison smiled. Hal had just confessed. He had to alert the others. He knew that he couldn't TP to the desert because Hal had hacked the ability to TP. He called out to Princess Hannah and her family.

"Guys, I know where Hal is keeping his command blocks," he told them, and explained everything he had just overheard.

"We should keep someone stationed outside the jail to hear what they are talking about," suggested Anna.

"Good idea," said Peyton. "I'll go now."

Princess Hannah and her family were returning to the desert. She told him they would go to the desert dungeon and destroy the command blocks and stop the hacking.

"Once we have destroyed the command blocks, we will TP to you guys and let you know that the hacking is over," she said. Then she sprinted off to the desert with her family.

Andrew said, "Once the hacking is done, I want to go under the water and remove all of the treasures from the ocean monument and return them to everyone."

"I want to go with you," said Julian.

"Great," said Edison. "Once the command blocks are destroyed, we will be able to have peace in the Overworld again."

Billy smiled. "I never thought we'd have peace again. This has been one of the hardest cases we've ever worked on."

"And it's not over yet," said Anna. "They still have to destroy the command blocks."

Edison joined Peyton and stood outside the jail and waited for more confessions, but Peyton said the fighting had subsided and the trio was just getting used to their life in the small bedrock jail in Verdant Valley.

Edison and Peyton stood by the door and listened as they waited for Princess Hannah to TP back to them. It was getting dark, and they worried that they would soon be vulnerable to hostile mobs.

"Should we wait here?" asked Edison.

"I think we should head home," said Peyton.

When Edison entered his home, he hoped he'd see Puddles, which would be a sign that the command blocks were destroyed, but he didn't see his pet ocelot. He was so tired that he fell asleep the minute his head was on his red wool blanket. When he woke up, the sun was shining through the window, and he heard a familiar sound.

"Meow." Puddles was next to his bed and wanted breakfast.

18

REWARDS

Edison was elated to be reunited with his ocelot, but he was even happier when Princess Hannah and her family walked through his door.

"We destroyed the command blocks," Princess Hannah exclaimed.

Edison looked down at Puddles. "I can tell. Were you also reunited with Scooter?"

"Yes." She smiled. "I'm so glad all of this is over. And to think, I came to you because I was worried about my missing ocelot. Who knew that was just a minor problem compared to what was going on in the Overworld?"

"It was still a big problem. I know I was very upset when Puddles vanished due to Hal's hacking. But I'm thrilled you were able to destroy the command blocks," said Edison.

Billy rushed through the door. "Have the command

blocks been destroyed?" But he didn't wait for an answer. He knew they had been destroyed. He saw Princess Hannah and her family standing in Edison's living room.

"We wanted to invite you and your friends to a party in our desert temple today," said the king.

"We want to celebrate all you have done for us," added the queen.

"We'd love to go," said Edison, and he left to find his friends. He had to tell his friends about the celebration in the desert temple.

He TPed to Forest Haven and found Andrew and Julian preparing for their underwater journey. He told them about the party.

"Now that the command blocks have been destroyed and Hal's hacking is over, we have to travel to the ocean biome," said Andrew. "I don't think we have time for a party."

"The king and queen want to honor us for all of our help. I think it would be nice you go," said Edison.

Andrew nodded. "O! ll go for a little while."

Edison searched for est of his friends and informed them of the party in the desert. They all TPed to the desert temple and were delighted to see Princess Hannah standing by the temple with Scooter.

"This is my ocelot." She pointed at Scooter and then led them into the grand desert temple.

The king and queen had put together an elaborate dinner. There was music and dancing. As they danced, Anna and Billy walked over to Edison.

"You're still out of Nether wart, right?" asked Billy.

"Yes, I am. Although I do have a few bottles of potion of Water Breathing left. Andrew told me I should have another flash sale," replied Edison.

"We were hoping you'd join us on a treasure hunt," said Billy.

"Yes, we have spent such a long time solving all of these cases around the Overworld that I thought it would be nice to go on a good old fashioned treasure hunt just for fun," said Anna.

"I guess I can join you guys," said Edison, "but I can't go for too long because I want to work at my potion stand."

"We promise we won't have you traveling around on the treasure hunt for that long," said Billy.

As the trio talked, Andrew and Julian walked over to them. "I want to thank you for helping me stop Hal," said Andrew.

"We want to thank you for the same thing," laughed Edison.

Billy added, "We're glad we met you."

"I feel the same way," said Andrew. "Now we're off to return all of the stolen treasure. Please, let's keep in touch."

The group promised to always keep in touch, wished Andrew and Julian a productive trip across the Overworld, and watched their new friends leave the desert and go toward the shore.

The king and queen called for Edison, Anna, and Billy. They wanted them to see the large cake they had made for the celebration.

"It's chocolate," said Billy. "That's my favorite."

The gang feasted on cake, happy that they had solved another case and knowing that they couldn't have done it without their new friends, who they hoped they'd see again.

The End